Making a Mobile

Heather Hammonds
Photographs by Lindsay Edwards

Contents

Goal To make a mobile that will glow in the dark

Materials

You will need:

- flat cardboard
- a pencil
- scissors
- paint brushes
- yellow glow-in-the-dark paint
- cardboard rolls

- old CDs
- a ruler
- a ball of string
- silver foil
- a stick, 40 cm long
- 10 paper clips

Steps

1. Draw some moons and stars on the cardboard.

2. Cut out the moons and stars. Make a little hole with the pencil in each one.

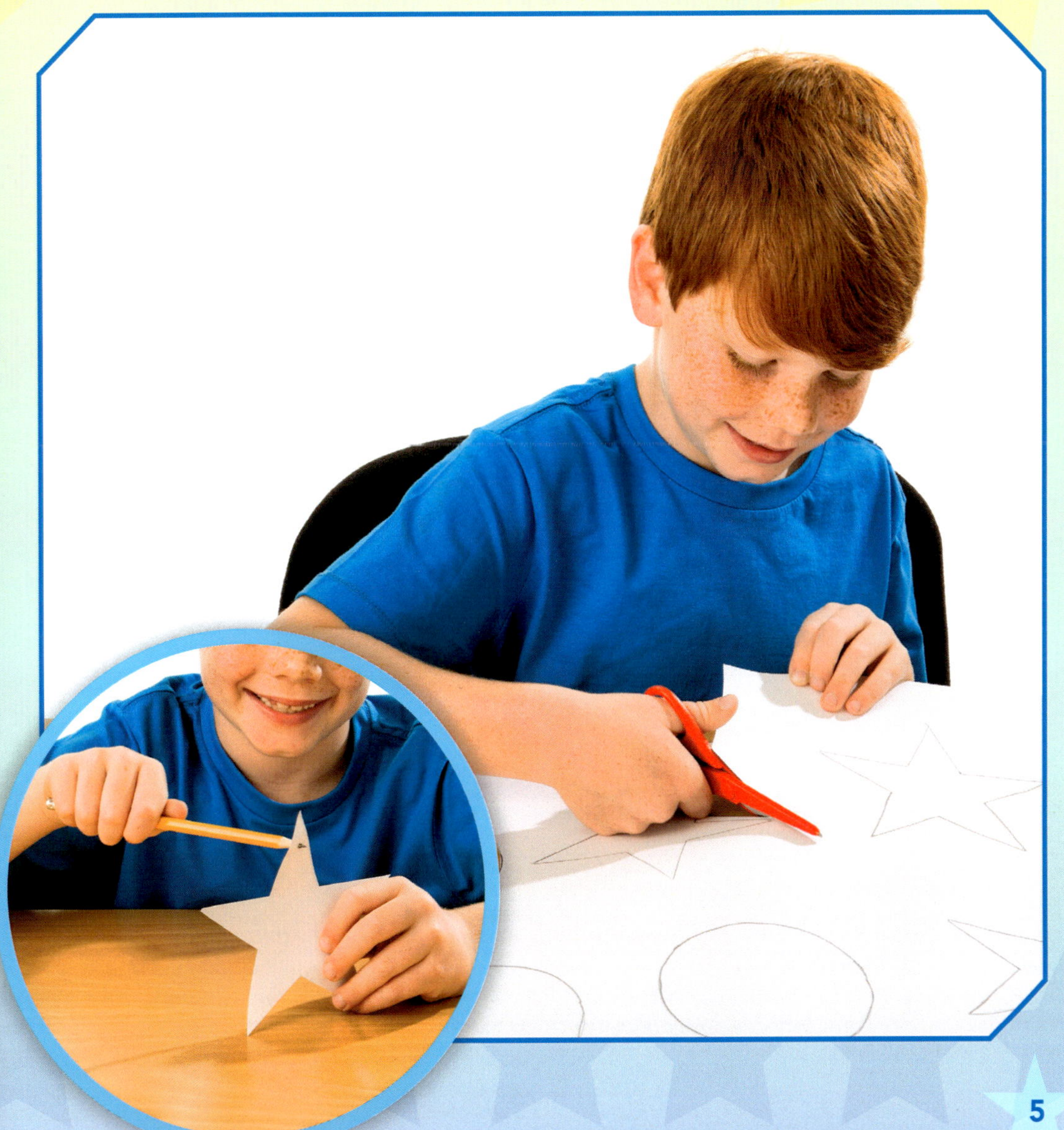

3. Paint both sides of the moons and stars yellow, with the **glow-in-the-dark paint**.

4. Paint some little moons and stars on the CDs and the cardboard rolls, too. Wait for the paint to dry.

5. Cut the string.
Make one bit 10 cm long.

Cut two more bits.
Each one should be 80 cm long.

Cut another two bits.
Each one should be 100 cm long.

6. Put some silver **foil** around the stick.

7. Put all the **paper clips** together, to make a long chain.

8. Tie the paper clips to the middle of the stick with the 10 cm bit of string.

9. Put a yellow star
onto each long bit of string.
Push the string through the holes in the stars.
Tie the string tight, so the stars stay in place.

10. Tie all the moons and CDs onto the bits of string, too.

11. Tie a cardboard roll onto the end of each of the strings.

12. Tie the strings with the stars, moons, CDs and cardboard rolls onto the stick. Mix them up so they look good.

13. Find a place to hang your new mobile. Put the mobile near a window where there is a lot of light.

When it is dark, all the stars and moons on your mobile will glow!

Glossary

foil	metal rolled into very thin sheets
glow-in-the-dark paint	paint that glows in the dark
paper clips	bent wire to hold sheets of paper together